Roadkill Confidential

A Noir-ish Meditation on Brutality

by Sheila Callaghan

A SAMUEL FRENCH ACTING EDITION

SAMUEL FRENCH

FOUNDED 1830

NEW YORK HOLLYWOOD LONDON TORONTO

SAMUELFRENCH.COM

ISBN 978-0-573-69923-8   Printed in U.S.A.   #29869

MUSIC USE NOTE

IMPORTANT BILLING AND CREDIT REQUIREMENTS

ROADKILL CONFIDENTIAL premiered at 3LD in September 2010 produced by Clubbed Thumb, an OBIE award-winning company that commissions, develops, and produces funny, strange, and provocative new plays by living American writers. The production was directed by Kip Fagan, with set design by Peter Ksander, costume design by Jessica Pabst, lighting design by Jeanette Oi-suk Yew, sound design by Bart Fasbender, video design by Shaun Irons & Lauren Petty, sculpture design by Jessica Scott, and properties by Miranda King. The cast was as follows:

RANDY/FRIZZY HAIRED MAN	Alex Anfanger
TREVOR	Rebecca Henderson
MELANIE	Polly Lee
FBI MAN	Danny Mastrogiorgio
WILLIAM/TV ANNOUNCER/DOCTOR	Greg McFadden

CHARACTERS

TREVOR – female, mid 30's, furtive and glamorous

WILLIAM / TV ANNOUNCER / DOCTOR – male, mid-late 40's, balding, dorky, well-meaning

RANDY / FRIZZY HAIRED MAN – male, 14, wiry and manic

MELANIE – female, late 20's-early 30's, bubbly and shrill

FBI MAN – male, 30's-40's, cool, level, mysterious, jaded

SETTING

A small New England county, upstate New York.
A road.
A dark nondescript room.

TIME

The end of fall, moving into the winter.

AUTHOR'S NOTES

The setting should not be real, or naturalistic. It should not be a set for the piece to play within but rather something against which the piece can resonate: more installation than set.

An ellipses is set within parenthesis is used to indicate a gesture or some sort of vocal sound appropriate to the character and the situation. It is not a realistic sound, however.

The installation will begin as something simple, but will transform throughout the play, perhaps during the transitions at the hands of Trevor, until ultimately the entire playing space and beyond is one enormous diorama.

PLEASE NOTE: Trevor is onstage for the entire duration. When not specifically noted, she is working and watching television, and reacting to it all. She is especially present on stage whenever FBI MAN is talking, whether lit specially, or in her own realm of movement and expression.

FBI MAN is also always present, always watching her, whether on his surveillance equipment, or in the room with her separated by the membrane of reality. He is the eternal voyeur. We must feel his desperation and obsession in every second of the play. We see the play THROUGH him, always.

All scene titles are projected.

Special thanks to Suli Holum, Birgit Huppuch, Sam Gold, Heidi Schreck, Jenny Morris, Hannah Cabbell, Carla Harting, Sheri Graubert, Polly Carl, Brooke O'Hara, Brendan Connelly, Laura Heisler, Amy Mueller, Bill Coelius, Dan Illian, Max Jenkins, Jeff Biehl, Sam Wright, Robin Lord Taylor, Andrew Dolan, Mark Shanahan, Teddy Bergman, Gibson Frazier, Danny Manley, Matt Maher, Mather Zickel, Reed Birney, Adam Farabee, Darren Pettie, Joel van Liew, Alex Anfanger, Maria Dizzia, Ana Reeder, Rebecca Henderson, David Brooks, Sarah Leonard, Matthew Macquire, Christina Kirk, Steven Kurtz and the Critical Ensemble, Seth Glewen, Adam Greenfield, The Playwright's Center, the MAP Fund, Playwrights' Horizons, Diana Konopka, Meg MacCary, and The Millay Colony.

FBI MAN. You could say it all began a month ago

But that's not where I'll start
I'll start *before* it started

On a radiant Tuesday morning
In the lazy days of late spring

Trevor was contemplating her next project.
She didn't know what form it would take
Nor how much time
Nor even what material
She only knew
It was to be brutal.

(**TREVOR** *is in her studio, watching TV news, as she does throughout the play.*)

Who is Trevor, you ask?

She might have been my greatest triumph.
But she was my demise.
So to speak.

(**TREVOR** *flips the channels. Lots of violence. She settles on one station. A* **TV ANNOUNCER**'s *voice is heard.*)

TV ANNOUNCER. And in sadder news
A child has died in the Berkshires this week
Seven year-old Callie Stewart touched a wild bunny
Outside her home in Austerlitz
The animal was infected with a rare bacterial disease
Causing Callie to perish within mere days.
The name of the disease is being withheld
For reasons of national security

But let it be known, Berkshire residents
The bunny has been detained.
You are in no danger.

(**TREVOR** *is suddenly in her car, driving.*)

(*THUMP. Squeal of tires. She pulls over.*)

(*She has hit a bunny accidentally. She stares at it. Emotion: compassion revulsion fascination etc.*)

(*She retrieves a camera and photographs it dying. Then – she gets an idea. She puts on a pair of work-gloves.*)

FBI MAN. Jump cut.

Five months later

Trevor's in bed with a frizzy haired man.

ONE MONTH AGO: RUBBER FACE

(**TREVOR** *is in her studio, now in bed with her lover, a frizzy-haired man. They are frozen.*)

(*The* **FRIZZY-HAIRED MAN** *is playing with* **TREVOR**'s *face.*)

(*Everything around them is covered in tarps.*)

(**TREVOR** *is staring at a flickering TV with the sound off. She wears a tie and white shirt.*)

FRIZZY-HAIRED MAN. Rubber-face

TREVOR. I'm trying to think of way to tell you to stop that
Without using the words "aggravating" or "retarded"

FRIZZY-HAIRED MAN. Ha!
Sorry.
I'll make coffee?
Should I make coffee?

(*He finds a piece of paper.*)

What is this?

(*He reads.*)

Friendly Fire
The Roadside Explosives
Mortar Rounds
The Drive Bys
The Ethnic Cleanse
Checkpoint Fuckyou

TREVOR. Band names

FRIZZY-HAIRED MAN. Who's in a band?

TREVOR. No one
I couldn't sleep.
Nightmares
My hands were like this the whole time

(*He flips the paper over and reads.*)

FRIZZY-HAIRED MAN. "Thanks for the help. You're a swell
  kid. Sorry it didn't work out. With Affection, Trevor."

TREVOR. That's from yesterday
  I thought you were leaving much sooner

FRIZZY-HAIRED MAN. What did you eat for lunch yesterday

TREVOR. Why?

FRIZZY-HAIRED MAN. Because sometimes what you eat
  Like eating badly affects your dreams
  The shattering of one's self-image

TREVOR. You're much cuter when you're focused on pleas-
  ing me

FRIZZY-HAIRED MAN. I need a little break
  My jaw hurts

TREVOR. All right
  I'll tell you what I dreamed, then

FRIZZY-HAIRED MAN. Please

TREVOR. I was the keeper of the marvel

FRIZZY-HAIRED MAN. Wow.
  You aren't ordinary.

TREVOR. I know.

  *(**FRIZZY-HAIRED MAN** kisses **TREVOR**. He is about to
  turn off the TV.)*

TREVOR. Don't touch that.

FRIZZY-HAIRED MAN. Okay
  I'm so happy to be here –

TREVOR. What about my coffee?

FRIZZY-HAIRED MAN. Right.
  Sorry.

  (He stands.)

  Ow.

TREVOR. Your back
  Poor thing
  I have advil

FRIZZY-HAIRED MAN. They were heavier than I thought
  Are you using more wood, or

TREVOR. Metal

FRIZZY-HAIRED MAN. Oh my gosh
  I can't wait to see them
  This is so huge for me, Trevor

TREVOR. I know, baby

FRIZZY-HAIRED MAN. I mean the first time I
  Your opening at the Whitney

  I mean visceral and dark but um with
  Like this brutal intimacy
  And so fucking beautiful
  I'd never / seen anything

TREVOR. Okay why not drive back to campus
  And yammer from the comfort of your dorm room

FRIZZY-HAIRED MAN. Oh.
  But just a second ago –

TREVOR. I changed my mind.
  Go now.

FRIZZY-HAIRED MAN. Okay.
  Um.
  Need me to move anything else?

TREVOR. No thank you.

FRIZZY-HAIRED MAN. Okay.
  (…)
  Want a sandwich
  I can get you a sandwich

TREVOR. Good lord.

FRIZZY-HAIRED MAN. Could I just see one of them?
  I won't take a picture or anything
  See?
  Here's my cell phone
  I'll leave it / over there

TREVOR. You're about to make me into someone
        Who demonstrates incredibly bad romantic judgment

FRIZZY-HAIRED MAN. Well I helped you and everything
        And we did have pretty okay sex

TREVOR. Okay.
        a) No one sees these until they're done, not even my
        husband
        b) Dignity, maybe? and
        c) Goodbye. Truly.

        (He hesitates.)

FRIZZY-HAIRED MAN. (…)
        I fucked up.
        I peeked beneath the tarp

TREVOR. When

FRIZZY-HAIRED MAN. Just for second
        I saw fur

TREVOR. Did you touch it?

FRIZZY-HAIRED MAN. Just for a second
        I couldn't help / myself

TREVOR. You touched it

FRIZZY-HAIRED MAN. Hardly, it was more like a

TREVOR. With the gloves on?

FRIZZY-HAIRED MAN. I took them off

TREVOR. Oh God

FRIZZY-HAIRED MAN. Just for a second

TREVOR. You idiot
        I said not to touch it

FRIZZY-HAIRED MAN. I know

TREVOR. I said "don't touch the art"

FRIZZY-HAIRED MAN. Nothing broke or

TREVOR. "hold the base by the straps"

FRIZZY-HAIRED MAN. The glue / was

TREVOR. Why did you touch it

FRIZZY-HAIRED MAN. DRY, okay

    I didn't even SEE anything

    I just FELT it

TREVOR. Oh God

FRIZZY-HAIRED MAN. Trevor

TREVOR. Oh God

FRIZZY-HAIRED MAN. Trevor

    I'm sorry

    Please

TREVOR. (…)

FRIZZY-HAIRED MAN. What was the exact crime

    Let me understand

TREVOR. Get out.

FRIZZY-HAIRED MAN. Trevor, I'm a –

    Please don't be mad

    I'm not like those freaks on the lawn with the camcorders

    I'm a fan Trevor but I'm not disgusting

    I'm not

    I'm not

(**Something beautiful and violent and dramatic happens to **TREVOR** *here.* **FRIZZY-HAIRED MAN** *does not hear or see her. Maybe he has disappeared, or is frozen.)*

*(***TREVOR** *drives home from her studio. She wears special gloves.)*

(She hits several small animals along the way. THUMP. THUMP. THUMP.)

(Each one she hits she stops and retrieves, with compassion and horror. Some of the animals are still alive.)

(It is a dance; the Hit Animal Dance.)

(It is funny.)

(meanwhile….)

FBI MAN. Later that night

   I got a disturbing phone call

   (He gets a phone call. He answers it.)

   Yello.

   (…)

   Uh-huhm.

   (…)

   Uh-huhm.

   (…)

   Uh-huhm.

   (…)

   Uh-huhm.

   (…)

   I'm there.

   (He hangs up.)

   Hospital upstate.

   A matter of national security

   And so it begins.

THIS COULD BE THAT

(The **FBI MAN** *stands next to a* **DOCTOR**.*)*

(They both stand over the corpse of the **FRIZZY-HAIRED MAN**.*)*

(The **FBI MAN** *reads from a small piece of paper in a plastic bag, which he handles with rubber gloves and tongs.)*

(The **DOCTOR** *is very, very nervous. He keeps looking over his shoulder.)*

FBI MAN. The Drive Bys
  The Ethnic Cleanse
  Checkpoint Fuckyou

DOCTOR. Was in his back pocket
  Admitted this morning
  Dizziness, fatigue, fever
  We assumed it was a severe pleuropneumonic infection
  Dangerous but not enough to, um
  But then we found that paper
  So we did some tests
  By the time we figured it out, well
  (…)
  Rapid diagnostic testing is not widely available for this

FBI MAN. Uh-huhm

(He revolves around the body, examining it, like a dance.)

DOCTOR. We are so glad you are here
  The disease is called "tularemia"
  "Rabbit disease"
  S-sm-smaller mammals act as reservoir hosts
  Prairie dogs, hares, muskrats, squirrels, voles
  Humans can contract it several ways
  Through ticks or flies or mosquitoes
  Or by handling the meat and skins of infected animals

FBI MAN. Uh-huhm

DOCTOR. Or um

> From food or water that has been contaminated
> Or through the air
> If um, sprayed

FBI MAN. Uh-huhm

DOCTOR. Um

> Symptoms include:
> Rapid onset
> Sudden fever
> Headaches
> Muscle aches
> Diarrhea
> Joint pain
> Dry cough
> Progressive weakness
> It's one of the m-m-most infective bacteria known to m-m-man
> What, um, what

FBI MAN. It was used by the Russians during World War II

> Before that by the Japanese against Manchuria
> The US developed strains of the disease in the 50's
> Part of their biological warfare program
> Terminated in the early 60's
> When used as a weapon
> The defense department classifies this
> As a category 8 agent

DOCTOR. Wow

> Um

FBI MAN. The disease cannot be spread from person to person

> It infects through mucous membranes, the gastrointestinal tract, the lungs
> The skin

DOCTOR. We have no vaccine
    Everyone is so paranoid around here
    We sent the receptionist home
    The nurses think we moved him to CPU

FBI MAN. Good

DOCTOR. This
    Of course this could be a single incident
    Like Austerlitz
    The little girl
    Um
    This could be that
    If it weren't for the note

(The **FBI MAN** *takes off his Ray Bans and leans into the* **FRIZZY-HAIRED MAN***, to inspect him more closely.)*

(We see he has a long scar across one eye.)

(a beat)

He was twenty-one
He was a student

(The **FBI MAN** *returns his glasses to his face and looks at the back of the letter.)*

FBI MAN. "With affection
    Trevor"

(The **DOCTOR** *disappears.)*

(The **FBI MAN** *is in a spotlight, thinking. A dramatic moment for him. Maybe music.)*

(He opens his cellphone. Dials a few numbers. Into the receiver:)

It's time.
How soon can you get it to me?
Perfect.

(to us)

I won't lie
I'm at my best

FBI MAN. *(cont.)* When the fate of the nation is at hand
Domestic situations however are not my specialty
International was always my bag

(He opens a trunk of costumes.)

(He dons an exterminator's outfit, "Bugs B-gone," and a cap.)

Like any good agent
I adapt.

Voila.
Upstate New York.
Mission?
Discover whether or not target is knowingly utilizing
A classified biological weapon
For the threat toward and/or destruction of human life

So I motored up to Albany
Got myself a shitty, heatless efficiency
the heart of the Hudson Valley
And readied myself for the ride

(meanwhile....)

PRUNE CEDARWOOD

(WILLIAM, MELANIE, TREVOR, *and* RANDY *are all seated at dinner.*)

(MELANIE *is a little giddy and tipsy.*)

(*She is dressed elegantly.*)

(TREVOR *is unreadable, but slightly on edge.*)

(RANDY *eats in complete silence. He wears headphones.*)

WILLIAM. *(sipping wine)* Prune
Cedarwood
Um

MELANIE. As a rule I'm not a red wine person but *this*

WILLIAM. The fellow recommended it /
A little oaky, but

MELANIE. Mmmmm
Okay
Should we toast?

WILLIAM. To…

MELANIE. Trevor's new series?

TREVOR. Well that's swell of you Melanie
But how can you toast to something you can't possibly grasp?

(slight beat)

Having not seen it, of course.

MELANIE. Oh I know!
To the first of many neighborly dinners!
Thank you for having me, Trevor

TREVOR. Well you just kind of stopped by –

MELANIE. But you didn't have to let me in!

TREVOR. That is absolutely true.
Cheers.

(They drink. The doorbell rings.)

WILLIAM. Well gosh, now who could that be?

(**TREVOR** *gets it. It's the* **FBI MAN** *in his exterminator's outfit.*)

TREVOR. Exterminator

FBI MAN. Keep eating
I'll find my way around

(*No one looks at him.*)

(*He winks theatrically at us, then begins to inspect the house. He surreptitiously scrutinizes door hinges and vents.*)

MELANIE. Do you have vermin?

TREVOR. Just bugs
Flies mostly.

WILLIAM. 'Tis the season!
Right?

TREVOR. My studio in the woods is filled with 'em
They buzz around in circles like drunken pilots
They know they're supposed to be dying
Their bodies tell them so
But it's not cold enough to knock them out
So they kinda just flail around in a hazy purgatorio
until their engines peter out
Pretty soon my window sill will be covered
in a writhing pile of half-dead insects.

(**MELANIE** *finally notices* **RANDY**.)

MELANIE. He certainly does enjoy his forks!
(…)
Ohhhh!
A lyric just popped into my head.

Red redwiiiiiiine
Goes to my heeeeaaaad
Makes me forget that I'm

No no wait it goes:
Red redwiiiiiiine

MELANIE. *(cont.)* Stay close to me
 Don't let me be alone
 Just mrahmrahngarahnga
 And then there's a rap, I can't remember
 Didn't you two used to make wine?
 When Trevor first moved in?

 (to **TREVOR***)*

 I remember you on your knees picking grapes outside
 You were so young!
 I asked what you what you were doing
 You said "we're making wine"
 But my brain heard "we're making love"
 I was so ashamed –

WILLIAM. *(suddenly remembering)* Ah!

 (rapping)

 Red red wine you mek me feel so fine
 You keep me rockin' all of the time

MELANIE. *(delighted)* Yes!

RANDY. Dad.

WILLIAM. *(feeling a little foolish but going for it)* Red red wine
 you mek me feel so grand
 I feel a million dollar when yajusin ma 'and

MELANIE. It's like a code!
 Keep going!

WILLIAM. *(uncertain)* Red red wine you mek me feel so sad
 Any time I see ya go it mek me feel bad

RANDY. Dad! I'm eating!

WILLIAM. *(uncertain)* Red red wine you mek me feel so fine
 Monkey back and moosaban a sweet ep line

MELANIE. WHAT?!

WILLIAM. *(getting into it)* Red red wine you give me oleeba-
 zing
 Oleeba-zing mek me do me own ting

MELANIE. *(applauding)* Yay!

WILLIAM. I'm sweating!

MELANIE. That was AMA/ ZING

WILLIAM. *(out of breath)* We used to
in grad school
we'd play it over and over
ah

MELANIE. Do you need some / water?

WILLIAM. I have the spins
I'm okay

> *(***MELANIE*** *pours him some water.)*

> *(They all freeze.)*

> *(Spotlight on the* **FBI MAN.***)*

FBI MAN. Indulge me a moment

> *(He removes a tiny platinum box from his jacket pocket and smiles broadly.)*

> *(He opens the lid and carefully dips his pinkie into the box. He shows us something practically invisible on the tip of his finger.)*

See this?

> *(He walks into the audience. He confides in us. He whispers to us, cajoles us. Flirts.)*

Too small?

Could be nothing, even?

A grain of sand, a flake of paprika?

A freckle?

Pin prick from a tailoring misadventure?

Ball-point pen mark?

Insect dropping?

Rat ovum?

I could go on....

FBI MAN. *(cont.)* Well it isn't nothing
Not by a longshot
What you don't see here
Is a two hundred MILLION dollar piece of surveillance equipment

(He scrutinizes his pinkie.)

Quadruple the signal-to-noise ratio and lux sensitivity of any previous machine close to its class
double the TVL and an optional ten thousand frames per second
thermal/infrared sensor fusion
multi-spectral nighttime imaging
360 degree non-angular field of view
rapid scan frequency
an UNLIMITED operation temperature – records data whether you're at the north pole or the gates of hell
half-mile operating distance
AND
Ninety-eight percent accurate color reproduction

You know how many of these exist in the world?
You're looking at it
Sui generis.
Version one-point-zero.
Classified top secret hush-hush sub-rosa.

You know who they give this to?
No one.
It's never been used.
Tested only twice by the husband-wife team who developed it
Stowed in a platinum box in a crystal drawer in a steel vault in an iron bunker
Dug a hundred miles down into the deep dark molten heart of the earth
Where it was kept for precisely twenty weeks

FBI MAN. *(cont.)* After which time it was removed
    And placed directly into my care.
    Three hours ago.

    (He places it carefully into the platinum box.)

    Why give it to *me*, you ask?
    I seem like an ordinary fellow.
    Hygienic but not suspiciously so
    Decent taste in footwear
    Marginally fit on a good day
    A sheen of competence akin to a mid-level executive

    I am not an opera
    I am not a threat
    I'm a block of clay-shaped clay
    I could even be you

    So.

    Why is it *me* holding this tiny precious box?

    The simple answer?
    Because I'm a patriot.

    *(He drops his trousers. Beneath, he wears American flag
    boxer shorts.)*

    I realize I have not given myself a proper introduction.
    I'll do so via an oblique anecdote

    These under-wears were a gift from a lady-friend
    Who, it turns out, was too much lady
    And not enough friend.

    One pair from a set of five.
    On the day she bought them
    She had gotten her hair permed
    She asked me to smell it
    I did
    pressed my face into her new curls
    the chemicals burned my eyes, nose, and throat
    I stayed there for a very long time

FBI MAN. *(cont.)* Burning

Because my loyalty to her was unwavering and bottom-less

And the pain was but a small consequence.

(a beat)

Precisely forty-seven weeks after the perm

I was called away for my job

Far away

When I returned, I was a few parts short

A fingernail

A toe

(He removes his glasses.)

An eye.

(a beat)

I told my lady friend how I had spent my time away

But ladies don't like to hear such things

Ladies prefer to imagine their sojourning mates, oh,

Doused in sunshine

sipping fruity drinks...

Not suspended from ceilings

Beaten with chains

Shocked with batons

Or injected with drugs.

(He pulls up his trousers.)

My position often requires long bouts of reflection

Which, at this point, led me to two conclusions:

One:

As unwaveringly loyal as I was to my lady friend

I am precisely five hundred times more loyal to my job.

And two:

(He places his glasses back onto his head.)

I am bottomless.

FBI MAN. *(cont.) (He retrieves the tiny box again and peeks inside.)* Did I mention this is water-proof?

(The scene unfreezes and **FBI MAN** *continues to work.)*

*(***FBI MAN** *addresses the room.)*

Critters like hinges and ducts

Warm places

You got an animal, animals?

Rodents, rabbits, prarie dogs? Voles?

WILLIAM. No –

MELANIE. Unless you count the ones in Trevor's Art Project

But they're all dead so maybe they don't count?

I don't know what I'm talking about

FBI MAN. All right.

MELANIE. I was thinking about going on the President's hike

Or maybe the trolley museum

We could pick apples

WILLIAM. Trevor's allergic to apples

MELANIE. REALLY???

MELANIE.	**WILLIAM.**
Wow.	Yes.
Wow.	Her throat constricts
Constricts?	

TREVOR. Imagine you're standing at the top of a steep hill

Wearing a pretty scarf

One end of the scarf is tied to a tractor in neutral

The other end is being pulled by someone who doesn't like you.

That's what it feels like.

MELANIE. (…)

And the film festival!

We need to get tickets early

This controversial movie about child prostitution in Cambodia

I'm not really interested but it sounds like something
you might like

TREVOR. Well Melanie

It's been a real pleasure

I'm so happy you stopped by

You are a stunning conversationalist

And have flawless skin

MELANIE. You're leaving?

TREVOR. I need to get back to work

MELANIE. I brought blueberry crumble!

I made / it!

TREVOR. Goodnight everyone

Don't need me for a few hours

MELANIE. Okay.

We'll save you a piece

TREVOR. Thank you

(*TREVOR exits. We see her in her studio, working, fretting.*)

(*an odd beat*)

WILLIAM. Hey Randy.

How's Dr. Fredrick working out?

(*to* **MELANIE**)

He's the highest rated adolescent therapist in the count…

(*RANDY exits, to his room, where he fight/dances.*)

(*A beat as* **MELANIE** *and* **WILLIAM** *eat.*)

WILLIAM. (*cont.*) Why did you come over, Melanie?

MELANIE. Crumble.

(…)

I wanted to get to know her a little better

WILLIAM. Why?

MELANIE. What do you mean, why? She's Trevor Pratt.

(*beat*)

Do the dead animals bother you, William?

(*small beat*)

WILLIAM. Of course not.

(**WILLIAM** *freezes..*)

(**FBI MAN** *pulls out a much-folded piece of paper from his wallet.*)

(*He reads.*)

FBI MAN. "Dear You."

"Hi. This is an asignment" – one "S" – "from Mrs. Katzler's 8th grade comp class. Otherwise I wouldn't be doing it.

"You're now 40. You are probably married and divorced and married again. You have a dog and a cat and a kid from each marriage, and they all hate you. You like your wife fine but she doesn't hump you anymore. You stopped smoking maybe, or you have a stash in your basement that you secretly." ?? "You are not a millionaire. But you're a boss of something lame. I think you drink. You having an affair with the secretary.

"You won't remember me, so here: I'm quiet. I'm taller than the other kids. I smoke. I eat alone. I like Jennifer Schultz and I touched her ass once. I have brown hair. I watch a lot of TV."

"Times up. Bye."

"Love,
you."

(**FBI MAN** *folds up the paper again and smiles at us.*)

FBI MAN. (*cont.*) One of the myriad reasons I was hired for this job – "hired" being the loosest of terms in a rogue operation – is my ability to spelunk the deepest recesses of an individual's psyche.

I spent seven years in the sacred mountains of Japan

Eating soybean paste and loquats

Studying the ancient martial art of Kory

Re-acquainting myself with myself

They said they needed to ease me back in

Fine, I said
Just give me what you got
And I'll show you what I am.

(gestures to the folded paper)

I wrote this letter to myself at 13. I saved it not because I have a special misty-eyed nostalgia for the myopia of youth, but because I thought I might need to remind myself that I once aspired to mediocrity.

And why do I invoke it now, you ask?

Exhibit A.

*(He gestures to the frozen **WILLIAM**.)*

*(Spotlight on the frozen **WILLIAM**.)*

William Whiting
44
Art historian
Sweats a lot
Has a fondness for cardigans
Never learned to swim
Was not in the car when his first wife died
Drinks tea with milk and sugar
Broke his nose once walking into a wall
Enjoys sad songs
Buys used books
Thinks it would have been "cool" to be a knight
Wishes his car were cleaner
Thinks his butt is squeezable
Hates cellular phones

*(Does an incredible, eerie impression of **WILLIAM**.)*

"A little oaky, but
Red redwine you mek me feel so fine
Trevor's allergic to apples
Trevor's allergic to apples"

IT'S ON THE MIDTERM

(**WILLIAM** *appears at a podium, lecturing.*)

(**FBI MAN** *dresses into college student gear.*)

WILLIAM. And I hope you dug last week's lecture,
"Vito Acconci and the Aesthetics of Contemporary
Narcissism".

It's on the mid-term!

Okey dokey smokies

Today we're gonna hit two controversial and "killer"
artists

Guillermo Vargas and Trevor Pratt.

(…)

Guillermo Vargas

Costa Rican fella

Famous for tying a sick dog to a gallery wall

And allowing it to starve

Yikes, right?

Some say the dog was fed in off hours

Others say it scurried off in the night

But Vargas claimed it died from neglect

No one knows the truth, oooooh

But the *point* was to expose hypocrisy

Vargas accused those who expressed outrage at the
dog's treatment

Of ignoring the same starving dog in the street

(…)

Question:

If we knew the dog had survived

Would it change the way we feel about the work?

Which brings us to my former student

Trevor Pratt

WILLIAM. *(cont.)* As many of you know, Trevor and I
(...)

I am Pratt's legal partner

Heretofore to be referred to in the third person

Pratt's exhibit "Impact" eight years ago

For which she acquired massive notoriety overnight

*(**WILLIAM** gestures to a series of slides as he talks:)*

(Of a car accident, and maybe life-sized photos hanging in a gallery, along with a blow-up of a police report and some other related documents. They are beautiful. Vivid colors. Blood.)

Photographs of a dead woman

Killed in a head-on collision

Priorly related to Pratt's partner by marriage

Pratt enlarged the images

And hung them

(Photo of a woman's body on asphalt. She looks like roadkill.)

Where did she find them?

On a shelf in the closet of her professor's bedroom
(...)

*(**FBI MAN** dons a baseball cap, a backpack, and a slouch.)*

(He raises his hand to ask a question.)

WILLIAM. Yes, in the front?

FBI MAN. Like, her professor gave her permission to use these photos
Why?

WILLIAM. Ah.

Excellent question

Was it an act of say, public mourning?

A poor decision in the throes of grief?

A fascination with the ethical implications?

WILLIAM. *(cont.)* Why not let us consider the larger question:

If we did not know the relationship of the artist to the subject

Would we still feel the emotional impact of the work?

I address this in my new book, actually.

(...)

which will be in stores.

(...)

at some point.

*(**FBI MAN** raises his hand again.)*

WILLIAM. Ah, yes?

FBI MAN. Like, do you think he regrets the decision?

WILLIAM. We can only speculate upon how he feels...

Although I imagine he...

(...)

Picture the kind of man

Who butters toast every day

Married to a woman

Who butters toast every day

Two toast butterers

Sitting in a butter-colored kitchen

Breathing together

For fifteen years.

Then

One toast-butterer

Gone

The other... listless, shellshocked...

*(Long beat. **FBI MAN** changes this scene with his eye... lights? Music????)*

*(**WILLIAM** crunches into himself.)*

WILLIAM. *(cont.)* And THEN

A tiny lanky creature reaches into the wreckage to touch him

Her hands get sliced by the shards

But she doesn't flinch

She isn't afraid of bleeding

Or even of pain

She is fear-less

Because she's the blade, you see

the blade fears nothing

It only cuts

I'd never been that close to a cutting-person

For me it was

she was…

Catechismic

I realized I could never butter toast again

I could only be cut.

(Sound stops. Lights normal.)

(We're back in the classroom. **WILLIAM** *straightens.)*

Um.

Theoretically speaking.

*(***FBI MAN*** raises his hand again.)*

WILLIAM. Yes?

FBI MAN. Is she working on anything right now?

WILLIAM. I will leave that to her people to divulge

FBI MAN. Aren't you her people?

(beat)

THINKING

*(**FBI MAN** is alone in his studio. Crappy smelly bed. Jammies. Gross unwashed coffee mug. Flickering bare bulb.)*

(He's thinking.)

FBI MAN. I'm just thinking.

(beat)

(He drinks from his coffee mug.)

This coffee has been sitting here for two days.
I could make a fresh pot
But I won't
I prefer stale bitter cold
I want to taste the rot
It helps me think

What kind of woman
I mean
It's just
(…)
You know?

I would say it's despicable
But I'm not here to judge
I'm here to probe, to sift, to root
To bore

You know I didn't even know she was famous
Until I googled her name.

I've been out of the loop.

However.
I'm no stranger to the capriciousness of the female mind.
My mother was a beauty queen
Miss University of Florida
I never saw her without make-up
Not even when she was drunk on the kitchen floor
Lying in the lap of someone who was not my father
While my brother and I cleaned up their vomit…

(a long long beat)

FBI MAN. *(cont.)* What was I saying?

> (**FBI MAN** *thinks, drinks more bad coffee, then turns on his monitors to watch the house.*)
>
> (*He watches an empty room for a little while. Music... We see his intense loneliness. Maybe he clips his toenails. Maybe he puts on lotion from a little blue jar. Maybe he does some crunches, some yoga stretches. It is a dance – the Sad Man Alone dance.*)
>
> (*suddenly:*)
>
> (**TREVOR**'s *face appears on the screen.*)

TREVOR. Hello?

> Exterminator?
>
> Did you put a teeny tiny camera in my house?
>
> A teeny tiny camera to watch what I'm doing?
>
> Are you watching me right now?
>
> (**FBI MAN** *stops breathing a moment.*)
>
> I'm used to it
>
> All eyes on me
>
> I thrive on it
>
> I'm a fucking narcissist after all
>
> I have an inflated sense of self-worth
>
> But somehow I feel invisible anyway
>
> You know that feeling?

FBI MAN. I do

TREVOR. You have an inflated sense of my worth too

> Otherwise you wouldn't be watching me right now
>
> Eating cereal
>
> Scratching my ass
>
> Getting drunk
>
> Peeing
>
> Let me know if I get boring

FBI MAN. I make no promises

TREVOR. I need to go now
    I need to work
    Will you be here when I come back?

FBI MAN. Yes

TREVOR. Good.
    Though I suppose you should know
    If you're looking for the hornet's nest
    You won't find it here

    (She exits.)

FBI MAN. Intriguing…
    I suppose she wants me to follow her.

    I don't "follow."
    I lead.

    *(***FBI MAN*** *tries to sleep. Restless.)*

    (Somewhere, elsewhere, **TREVOR** *is working, watching TV.)*

TV ANNOUNCER. And in local news
    A student has died in the Berkshires this week
    Twenty-one-year-old Benjamin Fizz
    Apparently he contracted the same rare bacterial disease
    Which claimed the life of young Callie Stewart.

    (Photo of the **FRIZZY HAIRED MAN** *somewhere, looking goofy.)*

    No need to panic, Berkshire residents.
    But please stay out of the woods
    And away from the squirrels
    And do not touch your pets without gloves
    And do not go hiking
    Or fishing
    Or swimming
    Or hunting
    Or birding
    Or leaf-peeping

TV ANNOUNCER. *(cont.)* And do not play outdoor sports
> And do not mow your lawn
> Or trim your bushes
> Or garden
> Or weed-whack
> Or rake
> Or hoe
> Until further notice
>
> Thank you.
>
> *(*TREVOR *panics.)*

TREVOR. I am fucked.
> I am fucked.
> I am fucked.
> I am fucked.
> I am fucked.
>
> *(then:)*
>
> *(The family appears for breakfast on the surveillance camera.* FBI MAN *wakes up and watches.)*

THEY FED ME VEGGIE BOOTY

(**WILLIAM** and **RANDY** *sit at the table eating corn flakes.*)

(**WILLIAM** *wears pajamas and reads the paper.*)

(**RANDY** *retrieves a briefcase and opens it. Inside is a fork collection. He considers his choices, then reaches for a tiny shrimp fork. He spears some sausages with it.*)

(*Ding-dong.*)

(**WILLIAM** *answers.*)

(**MELANIE** *enters wearing a fine-looking track suit and carrying two small sacks of coffee grounds.*)

MELANIE. Morning, starshines!

WILLIAM. Melanie –

MELANIE. Did you notice the roads are so empty the past few days?

WILLIAM. It's the rabbit scare

MELANIE. Oh.

Good thing I don't pay any attention to *that* fluff!

People get so worked up over nothing, don't they?

(…)

So.

I was going for my morning walk and guess what I found?

A coffee roaster right next to the library!

It's new!

Isn't that FABULOUS?

I don't drink coffee but I know you and Trevor…

Oh!

Is she sleeping?

(**TREVOR** *walks in wearing her lab coat.*)

TREVOR. Ah, Melanie, it's you

For a second I thought I was hearing

The sound of a large inflatable latex raft

Being squeezed through a tiny metal hole

MELANIE. (…)

So!

I know it's early

I was just passing by on my walk

I brought over some beans.

I hope you have a grinder!

May I?

(**MELANIE** *disappears into the kitchen.*)

(**TREVOR** *pours herself a coffee and sits.*)

(*Coffee grinding is heard. It hurts* **FBI MAN***'s ears.*)

(**MELANIE** *emerges again.*)

Well!

You're all ground up.

That's it I guess.

(…)

TREVOR. Would you like to stay for breakfast?

MELANIE. Oh no no no no

I was in the middle of my walk.

Eating defeats the purpose!

But maybe we could have tea soon?

Or pizza?

I don't really eat pizza

Or sandwiches?

Hundreds of options.

I mean we've been neighbors for so long

Let's start being neighborly!

Right William?

(*beat*)

WILLIAM. Thanks for the coffee Melanie

Very thoughtful

(*beat*)

MELANIE. Anyhoo.

Have a good morning!

(She exits.)

TREVOR. Think she's got an agenda knocking around that noggin
Or is it all impulse?

WILLIAM. Who knows.

(small beat)

You never came to bed

TREVOR. Sorry
I'm in hot pursuit

WILLIAM. That's cool, that's cool.
(…)
You sure there's nothing else?

TREVOR. Yeah, why?

WILLIAM. Dunno.
You seem a little
(…)

TREVOR. Um.

WILLIAM. Everything okay?

TREVOR. Yeah.
No.

WILLIAM. What is it?

TREVOR. Nothing.
Just some re-jiggering

WILLIAM. With the piece?

TREVOR. Yeah.
It's nothing.

WILLIAM. You sure?
Wanna talk it out?

TREVOR. I don't really know how, to be honest

WILLIAM. Just ramble.
I'll keep up

TREVOR. Okay, so.

> There's an element to it
> A very delicate, um
> That um
> Has the potential to get me into a lot of trouble

WILLIAM. With who?

> The police?

FBI MAN. Or with me…

TREVOR. Um I don't know maybe

WILLIAM. Thrilling!

> And controversial!
> Oh! Is this about all the disease hysteria?
> Are you addressing the cultural aggregation of paranoia
> in western consciousness?
> Sorry I'll shut up.
> Continue.

TREVOR. So my use of this "controversial" element

> May or may not have been ah.
> Leaked.

WILLIAM. So you're saying

> you built in an ideological trip-wire
> and it got tripped
> so its function has been prematurely fulfilled

TREVOR. Yeah.

WILLIAM. Are you in any trouble?

TREVOR. I don't know yet.

WILLIAM. Hm.

> Well
> (…)
> Could I just say something here?
> Without knowing the details?
> Maybe it's not about the piece itself, then
> Maybe it's about the *context*.

TREVOR. Huh?

WILLIAM. The *event* of the piece exists in the past tense, right?

So now it's a conversation about what was *intended*

Rather than what it *is*

We're talking about *meaning* versus *being*

It's performative almost

(TREVOR blinks uncomprehendingly. WILLIAM becomes increasingly excited, geeking out.)

So

The art IS the conversation

Or rather

The conversation is the art!

A bridge to further thinking!

Wow.

How elegant is *that?*

TREVOR. I sorta wish I could drive an auger down your neck

And crank it around

WILLIAM. I'm sorry

I know I'm not helpful

(…)

Just follow your instincts

RANDY. Are we gonna be famous again?

(small beat)

WILLIAM. Randy.

RANDY. Like last time

WILLIAM. You were six

RANDY. I remember

The lawn kids

The camcorders

They pitched tents

They fed me Veggie Booty

They took pictures of me

They took pictures of everything

(WILLIAM and TREVOR exchange nauseated glances.)

WILLIAM. It will be different this time

FBI MAN. Flashback: Fame Time.

(**Something immediate here – flashback to fame-time, or maybe just a whirlwind moment with music that demonstrates the headiness and brutality of getting famous overnight – violent and out of control.)

WILLIAM. *(cont.)* I need to shower
Good luck, muffin.

(He kisses TREVOR.)

And Randy
Kick ass at your audition

(He gives RANDY an awkward thumbs up.)

You're both superstars!

(He exits.)

(TREVOR is alone with RANDY.)

TREVOR. *(kind)*
Listen.
You need to be prepared.
This isn't a joke.
It *will* be different this time.

(small beat)

You're older now.
I want to know you can handle it.

Tell me you can handle it.

(RANDY explodes with some angry loud song, maybe "Gravedancer" by Pig Destroyer.*)

RANDY. *(sing-screaming)*
IN THIS TWO BEDROOM TOMB I'M SITTING ALL ALONE
WITH THE TELEVISION STATIC AND REFRIGERATOR DROOOOOOOOONE

---

*Please see Music Use Note on Page 3.

RANDY. *(cont.)* You don't scare me
    I broke into your studio
    Your stupid locks couldn't keep me out
    Some freaky shit, man
    Their eyes all bug

TREVOR. Did you touch anything?

RANDY. Sure
    Fondled all the girl rabbits
    Licked their little bunny twats.

> *(He mimes licking bunny twats. Then laughs. Then waits for the appropriate response from* **TREVOR.** *Which he does not get.)*

    Doesn't that make you wanna hurl?

TREVOR. Yes, Randy.
    I want to hurl.

RANDY. Heh.

TREVOR. Let me ask you something.
    How badly do you want to be famous?

RANDY. Enough to eat rabbit pussy

TREVOR. Enough to die?

> *(small beat)*

RANDY. The fuck does that mean?

TREVOR. Just a question –

RANDY. Die?
    Like –

TREVOR. *(carefully, touch of malice)* Because if you touched those animals
    You're already dead.
    But you're going to be more famous
    than you could ever imagine.

> *(***RANDY*** *is slightly terrified.)*

RANDY. I –

TREVOR. Did

    you

    touch

    them

    (*TREVOR and RANDY are quiet a moment. All we hear is the crunching of FBI MAN's popcorn.*)

RANDY. No.

TREVOR. What did you do?

RANDY. I looked through the window.

TREVOR. Say it again.

RANDY. I looked through the window.

TREVOR. Say it again.

RANDY. I looked through the window.

    (*beat*)

    I didn't look through the window.

    I didn't do anything.

    (*He is about to cry.*)

TREVOR. Okay.

    You did very well.

    You're a good little boy.

    You've earned a treat.

    I'll buy you some chocolate.

    Would you like that?

    (*RANDY nods.*)

TREVOR. Okay.

    Have another corn flake.

    (*They vanish.*)

FBI MAN. Wow!

    She's so mean!!

    Ha!

    It's nuts!

    But is she mean enough to kill?

FBI MAN. *(cont.)* I was famous once

>   When I was eleven years old
>   Our neighbor shot his wife
>   I stood behind the crime scene tape
>   Local news rushed over
>   Woman with a microphone asked what I thought
>   (…)
>   What *I* thought?
>   No one had ever asked me that
>   I said the wife deserved it
>   They aired it
>   My mother was so proud
>
>   Years later
>   After my brother's suicide
>   The cameras came to *my* house
>
>   I smiled for them

(Time passes. Perhaps we see more of the Sad Man Alone dance.)

(He thinks. He does other things.)

*(**RANDY** appears somewhere, still in his chicken leg, preparing for his audition.)*

FBI MAN. *(cont.)* That poor little mutant.

*(Spotlight on **RANDY**. Elaborate chicken dance.)*

>   Randy Whiting
>   14
>   No girlfriend
>   Has a fork collection
>   Could eat Doritos every meal
>   Lost his virginity last year
>   Collects vampire comics
>   Mother died when he was six
>   Likes to be clean
>   Ate a live beetle on a dare

Wishes his life were digital
Can't grow a mustache
Loves pizza bagels
Allergic to penicillin
Wishes he were famous

(**RANDY** *starts dancing as before. He is dressed as a chicken leg.*)

(*The* **FBI MAN** *dresses as a chicken nugget.*)

RANDY. You no longer have to deny your chicken cravings just because they strike at night
We now have more than 750 locations throughout the country
offering a special Late Night menu
Satisfy those cravings with favorites like
Lil' Snackers, Crispy Strips, Pop-its-

(*He stops dancing.*)

(*a beat*)

RANDY. Look at me.	FBI MAN. Look at me.
Look at me.	Look at me.
Look at me.	Look at me.
Look at me.	Look at me.

WHAT ARE YOU ANYWAY

(**RANDY** *is sitting in a chair wearing his chicken leg. He is chatting to the* **FBI MAN**, *still dressed as a chicken nugget.*)

(**FBI MAN** *is sharing a bag of Doritoes with* **RANDY**.)

(*They are at an audition.*)

RANDY. Fuckin' people
Thanks dude

(*long beat, with crunching*)

What are you anyway, dude?

FBI MAN. A nugget

RANDY. Oh. I thought you were a thigh.

(*Long beat. With crunching.*)

I'm sweating balls
This is a shit gig
Fuckin' costume smells like cheese dick

(**FBI MAN** *stares at* **RANDY** *strangely.*)

You wanna fuck me or sumpthin'?

FBI MAN. You look so friggin' familiar, dawg
Can't figure it out

RANDY. What about now?

(*Sudden screaming. And violent dancing.*)

MOVE YOUR BODY TO THE PUNK BEAT
WHILE POUNDING YOUR OPPONENTS
TO A BLOODY PULP

THIS GRUESOME DANCE GAME COMBINES
STREET-STYLE FIGHTING WITH
HARDCORE MUSIC
FOR INTENSE COMPETITION
AND BLOODSHED LIKE YOU'VE NEVER SEEN

FBI MAN. Holy shit!

>That was you!

>The "fan-mercial"

RANDY. Two hundred thousand hits, bro

>I was like a YouTube phenomenon

FBI MAN. You wore bike chains

>Black eyeliner

>Spiked hair

>And you had those contact lenses

>Gave you crazy wolf eyes

RANDY. OOOOOOWWWWWWWWWWWWWWW!

>It's a dope fuckin' game, man

>Ever play?

FBI MAN. Naw

RANDY. This gangster called Dwight

>He's a MENACE, right

>He owns everything

>Total terrorist

>And there's this chick, Ruby Sue

>She's a cage dancer at this punk club

>Basically he makes her his slave

>She's like chained to the bar

>And so it's your job to out-dance everyone in the club

>But also, you're beating the shit out of them

>Like crunk street fighting?

>>(**RANDY** *shows a move.*)

>Right?

>Different moves get different points

>>(**RANDY** *shows another move.*)

>Fiddy!

FBI MAN. Sucka!

>>(**RANDY** *shows another move.*)

>A hundy!

FBI MAN. Taste it! Taste it!

> (**RANDY** *shows another move. And another. It is horribly violent.*)

RANDY. And there's blood everywhere
Like the walls are drenched
And your eyeball is hanging by its optic nerve
And then you get to Dwight
And you have to slice him from chin to nuts
And once you've done that
You have the option of eating his heart

FBI MAN. Tight, tight.
Sounds fucking rad

RANDY. I had to stop playing it at home
My step-mom has a thing about violence or whatever

FBI MAN. She's pretty whack?

RANDY. Um
Dunno
She's got issues

FBI MAN. Who doesn't

RANDY. Right?
You probably know her
She's like, actual-world famous

FBI MAN. Dude, who is she?

RANDY. Trevor Pratt

FBI MAN. I know that name, bro…

RANDY. She's an artist

FBI MAN. Heeey
Didn't she have those pix of the car accident?
With the dead chick?

> (*small beat*)

RANDY. Yeah

FBI MAN. Oh snap
Dude, wasn't that your mom?

(beat)

RANDY. I wasn't supposed to see them
But they were like, everywhere
In the supermarket magazines
On TV

(**FBI MAN** *changes the scene with his eye...*)

I shat the bed
I scratched the skin off my cheeks
They took my TV
They made me bite a stick

FBI MAN. Why would your step-mom do that to you?

(**RANDY** *shrugs. He gets edgy, uncomfortable.*)

FBI MAN. Where does she work?

RANDY. In the woods somewhere.

FBI MAN. Where?

RANDY. Hey who are you man
Just some chicken thigh sitting here

FBI MAN. I'm a nugget, homes

RANDY. I don't have to tell you shit

FBI MAN. Just making conversation

RANDY. Whatever
Fuck this gig, man
I don't even need it
We're gonna be famous again
This time I'm not gonna fuckin cry in the corner
This time IT WILL BE SAVAGE

Thanks for the Doritoes

(**RANDY** *exits. Lights change back.*)

(**FBI MAN** *has a moment. He changes into his jammies again. He picks up the cold coffee from before. Music?*)

(**FBI MAN** *continues thinking, and drinking bad coffee.*)

FBI MAN. *(to us)* Shat the bed
    Bit a stick
    (!!!)

    Everything I learned about Trevor Pratt
    Turned my stomach one quarter turn more

    (Of course he is not revolted at all. Quite the opposite.)

    (He begins his nightly routine again, furiously.)

    Lack of empathy
    Total sociopath
    you're insane
    you didn't think showing a six year-old
    pix of his mom as roadkill
    would turn himloopy?
    A biological weapon in the hands of someone like her
    (…)

    (Brushes his teeth. Thinks.)

    I need to get closer to her somehow
    Peel back her rind
    Slice into her pulp

    But how?

    (Then. **TREVOR** *appears on screen again. She packs weed into a little bong. The lines of reality have begun to blur. Is* **FBI MAN** *in her space? Or is she in his?)*

TREVOR. Yo, exterminator.
    Wanna hit?

FBI MAN. You smoke grass.
    I might have guessed.

TREVOR. Stole it from Randy's closet
    He keeps it stashed in a little pencil case
    But never uses it
    He's a good kid
    Mostly

    Don't tell William I got high without him
    He hates that.

(She takes a hit. **FBI MAN** *leers.)*

FBI MAN. A dopehead, a thief, a terrorist AND a liar.
Watch the evils mount.

(to us)

Have I told you I have exceptional instincts?
I'm a divining rod for the morally bankrupt
Back in training they called me "Dognose"
Something to do with sniffing out corruption I suppose
They didn't like me

I wasn't there to win friends
I was there to destroy enemies
I'm a patriot goddamn it.

TREVOR. Can I tell you something?

This might be strange
I'm not afraid of dying

I'm afraid of …

I'm afraid of being anesthetized
by blasphemies of the flesh

FBI MAN. Anesthetized –

TREVOR. I think about it a lot

Sometimes?
When I've been watching those channels?

You know the channels
The ones with the machetes
And the bombs
And the guerrilla fighters
And the severed limbs

My chin gets all tingly
And I think, "Fuck!
It's happening!
I'm *numbing*"

And then I'm just like everyone else out there
The non-feelers

The ones who pass by a starving dog
And keep on walking

And then I think
Maybe that's okay
Maybe it isn't a crime to make oneself numb
To that kind of extremity
We're all human
We all have thresholds

And that's the exact moment
I want to kill myself.

(Beat. She laughs.)

I haven't been fucked in a while. Not well anyway.
Maybe that's my problem.

(She suddenly becomes deadly serious.)

I never meant to hurt him

FBI MAN. Who

TREVOR. He was so young.
I thought he wouldn't get it
The fuck do I know about kids
When he came home that day
After seeing the –

I looked into his eyes
His pupils were tiny
He kept saying
"That wasn't her.
That wasn't her."

He let me hold him.
He never let me hold him.

(beat)

I wonder why you haven't come for me yet
Maybe 'cause you like to watch

Or maybe you're like a python
Waiting to strike

FBI MAN. A python…

TREVOR. Or maybe you're just waiting to see

How far I'll go

I can tell you:

(She holds up a syringe.)

All the way.

(Long beat. Maybe **FBI MAN** *is sweating.)*

TREVOR. *(a whisper)* Come with me.

FBI MAN. Where are we going?

I need answers –

TREVOR. Bye.

(She exits. **FBI MAN** *is stunned a moment. He shakes it off.)*

FBI MAN. "All the way."

What could that mean?

(Jumpcut. Two nights later. **TREVOR** *is driving to her studio.)*

(Continues his nighttime grooming routine. Maybe he clips his toenails. Maybe he puts on lotion from a little blue jar. Maybe he does some crunches, some yoga stretches.)

(He tries to go to sleep in his drafty apartment with a threadbare blanket. We again see his hardship. His loneliness.)

(simultaneously:)

INTERLUDE:
TREVOR DRIVES FROM HER STUDIO

(**TREVOR** *drives from her studio.*)

(*She hits several small animals along the way. THUMP. THUMP. THUMP.*)

(*Each one she hits she stops and retrieves. But the dance is different this time. Not as funny.*)

(*Meanwhile,* **FBI MAN** *cannot sleep. He turns the surveillance camera on once again, and watches.*)

I HAVE COBBLER

(**MELANIE** *is wandering around the house clutching a peach cobbler.*)

(**FBI MAN** *watches.*)

MELANIE. *(cheerful)*
Hello?
Hello?
Anyone?
I have cobbler

(**TREVOR** *enters, gloves covered in blood.*)

TREVOR. Excuse the blood
I was flossing
Coco puff?

MELANIE. No, thank you.

(**TREVOR** *pours herself a bowl of Cocoa Puffs and munches the entire time* **MELANIE** *chats.*)

Goodness!
Well you've been a busy beaver haven't you!

Beaver
(???)

(**MELANIE** *hands* **TREVOR** *the cobbler.*)

TREVOR. Hey mind if I ask you a question?
What's with all this sloshing good will?

MELANIE. No reason!
It isn't even good.
The peaches weren't ripe
I ran out of sugar
I substituted cornstarch
I left the price tag on the crust
You can bring it to the barn later
I mean your studio
Ha!
I still think of it as a barn!

MELANIE. *(cont.)* Well.

    I'll put it here.

    (…)

    I'll just pop over later for the plate

FBI MAN. Where is the barn, Trevor?

MELANIE. Pop-over

    (???)

    (Long beat. **TREVOR** *returns to her Cocoa puffs.)*

    So how are things?

TREVOR. Pretty good

MELANIE. When do you think you'll be done?

TREVOR. Soon

MELANIE. Exciting.

FBI MAN. Exciting indeed…

MELANIE. So!

    So your work!

    Dead animals.

    (…)

    Gosh.

    (small beat)

TREVOR. Do they bother you, Melanie?

    (Long beat. **MELANIE** *struggles.)*

MELANIE. Be nice to have people around again

    The cameras, the snacks

    Never boring, that's for sure

    Ha!

    But.

TREVOR. You know, Melanie

    I think you might be my ideal audience.

    (a beat)

MELANIE. Really?

Oh my god.

Are you serious?

Oh my God!

I am so honored.

So very –

I'm having trouble finding the words

(…)

I'm calling it off with William

FBI MAN. WHAT?!

MELANIE. I'm deeply unsatisfied

We don't communicate

His mind drifts

Sometimes when we make love

He gives up in the middle

(a beat)

You knew, right

About him and me

TREVOR. No.   **FBI MAN.** No.

MELANIE. Oh.

It was only a few times.

Maybe seven.

We only talked a little

He talks more to me in his sleep than in life!

Sometimes he lectures

Sometimes he apologizes

To who, right??

FBI MAN. Melanie.

MELANIE. You know before you came along

We used to wave at each other

Him walking his dog

Me walking my cat

Hello, good morning, beautiful weather

Neighborly waving

MELANIE. *(cont.)* His wife too
> Hello good morning look at the leaves
> She looked so much like him
>
> Then you moved in
> And suddenly
> You were both on your knees with the grapes
> I didn't understand
>
> *(a beat)*

TREVOR. Why are you telling me this?

MELANIE. I have no one to talk to
> I think about you a lot.
>
> So!
> I'm ready
> To be friends
> What do you think?
> Could we do that?
>
> *(long beat)*

TREVOR. Hey Melanie
> Guess what?

MELANIE. What?

TREVOR. Go on!
> Guess!

MELANIE. What?
> I don't understand
> What am I guessing?

TREVOR. Just guess.
> Anything.

MELANIE. Okay.
> Give me a ballpark.

TREVOR. Guess what I think of you.

MELANIE. Oh!
> (…)
> Well I haven't a clue!

TREVOR. Don't even wanna try?

MELANIE. Well I suppose you think I'm cheerful?

And I have clean hair?

And you like my skin, you mentioned that the other day...

TREVOR. I think

That you are

A cunt.

(Stunned silence. Long beat.)

*(**TREVOR** bursts into laughter. A relieved **MELANIE** follows suit. So does **FBI MAN**. He changes into rustic gear.)*

MELANIE. *(laughing)* My goodness!

TREVOR. The look on your face!

You were all...

*(**TREVOR** mimics **MELANIE**'s look.)*

MELANIE. I *was!*

I *was* all...

*(**MELANIE** mimics **TREVOR** mimicing **MELANIE**'s look. The women laugh and laugh. Then they calm down.)*

TREVOR. Go away now

Get a haircut

MELANIE. Um

TREVOR. Buy a bright red belt

Take a long clarifying walk

MELANIE. Okay

You know

When everything blows over

I really do think we could be actual friends

*(**TREVOR** moves to the door and opens it for **MELANIE**.)*

TREVOR. Thanks for coming.

*(**MELANIE** is about to leave. She feels something odd, and turns back.)*

MELANIE. Is something about to happen, Trevor?

(They freeze.)

FBI MAN. Great question, Melanie.

Something IS about to happen, yes

What is it, Trevor?

Me
Infiltrating enemy lines
Me
The blood on your lab coat
The disease on your fingers
Me me me me

I'm gonna climb into your world
Snuggle up with your little "project"
And get nice and cozy

I will be so fucking close
You won't know where you end and I begin

We will become the ouroboros
Me the head, you the tail

And I will eat you alive.

*(**TREVOR** disappears.)*

Things just got personal.

*(spotlight on **MELANIE**)*

Melanie Colander
37
Divorced
No children
Has a silk scarf collection
Lives alone
Pees with the door shut
Loves jam
Reads tabloids
Takes a milk bath every Friday
Hates mold

Does not masturbate
Is not a good listener

(Does an incredible, eerie impression of **MELANIE.***)*

"As a rule, I'm not a red wine person.
I have no one to talk to
Dead animals
Is something about to happen, Trevor?
Is something about to happen, Trevor?"

ANYONE CAN MAKE THEMSELF HAPPY

(**MELANIE** *is on her knees in her garden, wearing garden-ing gear, silk scarf, fussy shoes, and a bright new red belt.*)

(**FBI MAN** *approaches, wearing his outdoorsy gear.*)

FBI MAN. Pardon me...
   I'm looking for Hill road?

MELANIE. You're on it

FBI MAN. Oh
   I didn't see a sign

MELANIE. It's blocked by the big "L"
   This used to be a horse farm

FBI MAN. Sorry to bother you

MELANIE. No bother
   I'm just murdering shrubs

FBI MAN. Your hole isn't deep enough
   Dig about four times the width of the root ball

MELANIE. Gosh!
   Are you a gardener?

FBI MAN. I dabble

MELANIE. You're like me!
   A dabbler!
   I love to dabble.
   You like to do nice things for yourself too, right

FBI MAN. I do

MELANIE. I knew it!
   It's a type
   Like, yesterday?
   I accidentally watched the news
   And I woke up in such a state!
   So I went golfing by myself
   I got to the course and I took off my shoes
   And lay my putter down
   And then I walked on the green grass barefoot

FBI MAN. Ooooh.

MELANIE. Cool and soft like a thick pile rug
    I walked and walked
FBI MAN. Mmmmmm.
MELANIE. And the other day?
    I made a cobbler
    The peaches weren't ripe
    I ran out of sugar
    I substituted cornstarch
    I left the price tag on the crust
    I can't make desserts
    I can't make anything really
    But it was fun!!!

    (**MELANIE** *zones a moment. She looks down at her bright
    red belt, touches it.*)

    (*Snaps back.*)

    You know?
    I think it's the small kindnesses one does for oneself that
    (...)
    It's my theory that I made up
    Close out the ugliness
    Close it out
    know what I mean?
FBI MAN. I do, I do
MELANIE. Because people, humans I mean
    Well there's a lack of elegance
    It's endemic
FBI MAN. Yes.
MELANIE. And overseas, the violence?
    Well what the heck's wrong with innocence
    For those of us who have the option
    Which is anyone, really
    ANYONE can make themselves happy
    So why not choose that
    Why WALLOW?
    I have a strict no-wallowing policy

FBI MAN. So smart.

MELANIE. This scarf is pure silk

    Jodie Foster is gay

    Are you married?

FBI MAN. Divorced

MELANIE. Me too!

    Well!

    Where are you from?

FBI MAN. Spencertown

MELANIE. What brings you over here?

FBI MAN. House for sale

MELANIE. Which one?

FBI MAN. 425?

MELANIE. Oh.

    You must have the wrong Hill road

FBI MAN. Google Maps, um

MELANIE. That house isn't for sale

FBI MAN. My realtor –

MELANIE. Who is your realtor?

FBI MAN. Missy… ah Missy….

MELANIE. *(distant)* Unless he put it on the market this morning, or…

    That's so strange

    He never mentioned

FBI MAN. I heard a famous artist lives there

MELANIE. Oh

    She's not famous any more

    Now she just scrapes dead animals off the side of the road

    Isn't that AWFUL?

FBI MAN. Why does she do that?

MELANIE. It's her art

    She keeps them in a barn

    She calls it her studio

FBI MAN. Is it nearby?

MELANIE. The barn?

Not really

It's pretty deep in the woods

Lot of dark windy roads –

FBI MAN. Where?

MELANIE. *(suddenly shy)* Oh.

It's private

FBI MAN. Could I

Could you

Forgive me

I'm not normally

But a famous....

MELANIE. She's working on something

I don't think she likes to have visitors there

FBI MAN. Of course not

Stupid of me

I've taken enough of your time

MELANIE. Not at all

*(A long beat. **FBI MAN** changes the scene somehow, with his thoughts, his eyes, his one bad eye...music?? Lights????)*

(dreamy) Sometimes?

In the market?

I stare at the packets of meat?

The loose blood in the cellophane?

And um

FBI MAN. Melanie

MELANIE. And yesterday I was driving at night

I hit something

I turned around to see if it was still alive

It was a possum

Scattered behind it was a handful of wet babies

(A long beat. Music off abruptly.)

FBI MAN. Thank you so much for the info
     You're a lovely woman

     (He kisses her hand gallantly.)

     Flawless skin

     (He hands her a card.)

     (Then he exits.)

     (She watches after him. Then freezes.)

     *(**FBI MAN** turns to us. He smiles.)*

     Bingo.

     (but then)

     That afternoon
     I got a disturbing phone call

     (He gets a phone call. He answers it.)

     Yello.

     (…)

     Uh-huhm.

     (…)

     Uh-huhm.

     (…)

     Uh-huhm.

     (…)

     Uh-huhm.

     (…)

     Evidence?

     (hand on the mouthpiece, to us)

     They're getting antsy.

     (back on the phone)

     Well it's a delicate –

     (…)

     I don't want to rush into –

     (…)

     She's a very –

FBI MAN. *(cont.)* (…)

I don't have anything concrete yet –

(…)

Buh-bye

(He hangs up. Miffed. Air quotes. Very angry.)

They're giving me a week.

A fucking *week* to determine malicious intent

And/or knowledgeable use of a controlled substance

For the purposes of –

They don't understand at all.

I hate that

I did not take on this assignment

For a hasty hacky bullcrappy –

(!!!)

I took it because I have questions

About human nature

About the desire to kill

About myself

Is a measure of artfulness

Too much to ask?

They don't understand the ineffable language of war

And this is war, my comrades.

A war of wills

(He flips on the monitors to watch **TREVOR.***)*

(But the camera no longer shows the house.)

(It has moved. It is dark.)

What the….

(He squints at the camera.)

My monitor –

(Lights brighten the screen. **TREVOR** *appears on camera. In her studio. Smiling.)*

TREVOR. Welcome.

> Figured I'd heat things up a bit.
>
> Hope you don't mind.

(She turns the camera a bit. Patch of fur, Set of eyes.)

FBI MAN. Ooohh

> Now you're playing with fire, sweetheart

TREVOR. This is my other home

> Meet the gang
>
> Dieter, Alan, Benzy, Justin, Veronika
>
> I spend more time with these guys
>
> than I do with my real family
>
> Does that seem sick?
>
> Well I am sick
>
> A little
>
> More than a little
>
> I'm not eating, not sleeping
>
> I can't feel here, here and here
>
> My instincts are totally tweaked
>
> I'm stuck
>
> I'm stuck
>
> And I don't have much time

> *(to camera)*

> Or do I?
>
> How much time do I have?

FBI MAN. Um…

TREVOR. Because this is driving me a little bonkers

> The not-knowing
>
> Waiting for the angry knocking
>
> The dudes in hazmat suits
>
> Helicopters, sirens
>
> I mean really
>
> What the fuck are you waiting for?
>
> This is a huge fucking deal
>
> A matter of national fucking security!

FBI MAN. Whoa, whoa, whoa
Slow down, game-changer –

TREVOR. I need help
I don't know what I'm asking for
I don't even know who I'm asking
But I'm –

I have no one
Just you
(...)

Can you help me?

(She freezes. Long beat.)

FBI MAN. Help her
Help her

But what about the rules?

(He smiles knowingly.)

Know what happened the last time I followed rules?

(He flips up his eyepatch dramatically)

Adiós a mis ojos.

(He flips it back down.)

(He dons a rain jacket.)

I would discover what the moment required
From within the moment itself

Mini-jumpcut. The next day. I had a date with destiny

(He douses himself with a bucket of water.)

NOT DEAD

(**TREVOR**'s studio.)

(Small light flicks on. **MELANIE** and **FBI MAN** enter. It is raining outside, they are damp, they shake out umbrellas.)

(**MELANIE** carries an open bottle of wine.)

MELANIE. Hee!

FBI MAN. Shhhhh….

MELANIE. Goodness
   Never broken into anything in my life!
   I feel WILD!!!

FBI MAN. Shhhhh!

MELANIE. You picked those locks like a pro

FBI MAN. I'm a contractor
   We get locked out of things a lot

MELANIE. Hee!
   This wine is making me,
   Whoooo!
   Okay now remember, if she comes by
   I'm here for my plate

FBI MAN. Thank you for bringing me here, Melanie
   You're a total doll

MELANIE. Oh, now –

FBI MAN. And so brave!

MELANIE. Oh stop.
   I'm really not brave
   I'm just drunk

FBI MAN. You know who you remind me of?
   Amelia Earhart

MELANIE. Shut up!

FBI MAN. You do!
   A fearless woman
   Plunging herself into unknown territory
   Very very sexy…

(FBI MAN nibbles on MELANIE's scarfed neck. She squeals.)

MELANIE. Do I smell nice?

It's a cinnamon spritz

I wanted to smell homemade

You still haven't told me what happened to your eye

FBI MAN. It's confidential

MELANIE. Man of mystery…

Hee!

Would you like a scarf?

I brought extra to cover the odor

(MELANIE giggles and takes out a scarf. She squirts a scent onto it.)

(FBI MAN takes it, holds it against his nose.)

Let's not be here too long…

FBI MAN. All right

Are you ready for lights, Amelia?

MELANIE. Oh my gosh oh my gosh

YES!

Do it do it!

(MELANIE shields her mouth with her scarf.)

(FBI MAN turns on an overhead light. MELANIE gasps. Both look around at all the work, which is half-uncovered.)

(FBI MAN is amazed. MELANIE is filled with horror)

I

Goodness

I

FBI MAN. My God

It's beautiful

(One of the animals twitches. MELANIE shrieks.)

MELANIE. AHHHHH!

Not dead!

Not dead!

(She runs to the FBI MAN*'s arms, hysterical. He comforts her and speaks to us.)*

(Suddenly, FBI MAN *has a stunning, awful, grotesque, yet perfect idea.)*

(He places a cloth over the plant.)

(to MELANIE*)*

FBI MAN. It won't hurt you

MELANIE. Why would anyone –
 It doesn't make any –
 I mean they're living breathing –

FBI MAN. Calm down –

MELANIE. It's HORRIBLE!
 It's HORRIBLE!
 You can't
 You can't kill things!
 You can't kill things and call it art!

FBI MAN. Why not?
 The world does it
 We all kill things
 In the name of other things

MELANIE. I want to go home

FBI MAN. If you show you're frightened
 You lose your advantage
 Do you want her to win?

MELANIE. Win?
 Win what?
 I don't / under

FBI MAN. Climb into her mind
 See what she's after
 Know your enemy

MELANIE. She's not my / enemy

FBI MAN. With empathy comes knowledge, Melanie
 I learned this as a contractor

 The best way to truly *know* a person
 Is to *become* that person

MELANIE. Oh dear

FBI MAN. Don't shut down like "Melanie"
Open yourself like "Trevor"
It's your only way in

MELANIE. N-now?
I don't think I'm quite / prepared

FBI MAN. *Now.*
Open yourself

(beat)

MELANIE. Open.

FBI MAN. Brave.

MELANIE. Open brave.

*(**MELANIE** takes a long drink of wine.)*

(Then she faces the animals.)

(She becomes trance-like.)

FBI MAN. What do you see

MELANIE. Their eyes…

FBI MAN. What else…

(Music, or sound, or noise begins to rise in the room, building. Or are the animals singing?)

MELANIE. *(dreamy)* I hit a possum the other day
I dreamt I ate its babies

(She is captivated. No going back.)

FBI MAN. If it moves you
You should touch it

*(**MELANIE** is very close to one animal. The animal turns its head to **MELANIE** a little.)*

*(**MELANIE** gasps a little.)*

(Her hand reaches out slowly.)

*(**MELANIE** touches the animal. Then strokes the animal.)*

*(**FBI MAN** flinches. But says nothing.)*

MELANIE. *(exhilarated, quiet)* He's warm

(…)

Oh my gosh

(She continues to stroke the animal.)

*(**FBI MAN** lets her. Face wrinkled with nausea.…)*

*(Something happens to **FBI MAN**. ??? Maybe **MELANIE** freezes, lights and music shift to reveal some turning point, or his inner turmoil at watching this. Or maybe not.)*

*(**FBI MAN** bursts from the scene…)*

WAS THAT NECESSARY

(During the following, **TREVOR** *drives to her studio. She wears special gloves.)*

(She hits several small animals along the way. THUMP. THUMP. THUMP.)

(Meanwhile…)

*(***FBI MAN*** *is doing angry pushups or situps, listening to his iPod. He is very very sweaty, shouting to himself over his tunes. Punishing himself.)*

(Unhinged a bit.)

FBI MAN. But it's important to keep this in mind:
Baseness may only occur
When the regulating force
Has become defunct

And I am a vigorous self-regulator

I do this with a frothing conviction
Press my nose to my own feces
And scream "WAS THAT NECESSARY?"
And if the answer is no, well…
Who is accountable?
ME.

(He smashes the iPod against his head.)

THE GOVERNMENT.

(smashes again)

A PATRIOT.

(again)

ME. ME. ME.

(Again again again. Then he throws it across the room.)

(A beat. He breathes, pulls himself together.)

It *was* necessary.
It was.
It was.

WHAT'S MISSING

(**TREVOR** *appears in her studio, working with a dying animal.*)

(**FBI MAN** *watches on the monitor.*)

(*She is outfitted in a chemical hazard suit. She handles a chemical in a syringe extremely carefully.*)

(*Only a few of the pieces are covered in tarps now.*)

(*She works and works. She talks to the animal.*)

TREVOR. Okay
This is gonna hurt like a motherfucker
Deep breaths

(*She injects a chemical into an animal. The animal squirms.*)

Shhhh
I'll sing you a song I've been working on
Yeah I wrote a song
It's a lullaby
It's called
"The Keeper of the Marvel"

(*She hums an intro. Then sings:*)

I'm the hmm hmm hmm –

(*stops*)

That's as far as I got.

(*The animal winces.*)

I know it's not much comfort right now
But try to remember:
You will be rewarded
When the doors are flung open

(*Then she is done.*)

(*She moves this animal with the others.*)

(*She evaluates all her work. The whole thing.*)

(*She is frustrated.*)

TREVOR. Shoot fuck balls.

FBI MAN. What's missing?

> (**TREVOR** *turns the TV on. War, violence. She pinches herself. She smacks herself in the face, pulls at it, etc. She's getting numb.*)
>
> (*She turns the TV off and paces a little.*)

Blasphemies of the flesh...

> (*knock on the door*)
>
> (**TREVOR** *removes her gloves and opens it.* **MELANIE** *is outside. She looks awful. She is coughing and hacking and shaking, and very weak.*)
>
> (**FBI MAN** *watches...*)

MELANIE. H – hello

I came for my plate

TREVOR. Jesus

Are you all right

> (**MELANIE** *stumbles into the studio. She wears sweats, heels, a scarf.*)

MELANIE. Bronchitis

I think

It's not contagious

Could I sit?

> (**MELANIE** *slumps in a heap of coughing.* **TREVOR** *grabs a chair and steadies her in it.*)
>
> (**FBI MAN** *watches...*)

TREVOR. You look / terrible

MELANIE. *(weakly)* So

How's William

How's he been

That's great

And Randy?

Oh, maybe next time

And you?

MELANIE. *(cont.)* Almost done?
Wonderful
Apples, crazy!
My shoes?
On SALE
Computers
Pants
Fruit cups
billiards
The animals
I wasn't expecting –
Their bodies were warm

TREVOR. Which / animals

MELANIE. I was here
Last night

TREVOR. You weren't here

MELANIE. I came for my plate

TREVOR. You couldn't have gotten in

MELANIE. He picked the locks for me

TREVOR. Who

MELANIE. I didn't come for my plate.
I came for um
Um
Um-um-um-um-um-um
(…)
Umpathy

(Coughing fit. **TREVOR** *notices the cloth over the plant.)*

TREVOR. Lay down
Over here

MELANIE. *(weakening)*
Anyhoo
You should –
We all should –
Have dinner, or
(…)

(**MELANIE** *closes her eyes.*)

(*long long beat*)

MELANIE *(cont.)* *(quietly)* Say something.

(**TREVOR** *opens her mouth to speak. War sounds?*)

TV ANNOUNCER. A three-vehicle convoy
was struck by a roadside bomb
80 miles outside the Gaza strip
seven Israelis were killed

(**TREVOR** *closes her mouth. She opens it. War sounds.*)

Then a bomb exploded
near a schoolhouse in Istanbul
fourteen Turkish children were killed

(**TREVOR** *closes her mouth. She opens it. War sounds.*)

Then two ethnic groups
clashed outside a church in Nairobi
twelve Kenyans were killed

(**TREVOR** *closes her mouth.*)

MELANIE. Why won't you say something
TREVOR. I just did
MELANIE. Something real

(*beat*)

(**TREVOR** *lays a pillow beneath* **MELANIE**'s *head.*)

(*She stares at* **MELANIE** *a moment.*)

FBI MAN. *(quietly)* Collateral damage.

(**FBI MAN** *moves toward her, unseen.*)

(*They sense one another.*)

(*They move around one another.*)

(*The "We Sense Each Other" dance.*)

Ho ho...
Look at you
The mistress stumbles into
The black widow's web...

(**TREVOR** *draws closer.*)

FBI MAN. (*cont.*) You're welcome.

(*a beat*)

(*a beat*)

At that moment

I got a disturbing phone call

(*He gets a phone call. He answers it.*)

Yello.

(…)

Uh-huhm.

(…)

Uh-huhm.

(…)

Uh-huhm.

(…)

WHAT?

(…)

I'm on it.

(*Closes his phone. To us. Utter disbelief, betrayal.*)

She bought two plane tickets to a foreign land

Leaving 9 pm tonight

(**TREVOR** *disappears.*)

(*miffed, pacing*)

She's leaving?

With whom?

And why?

When she's *this* close?

It doesn't make sense.

What am I missing?

What am I missing?

What am I fucking fucking missing?

(**FBI MAN** *dons autumnal camouflage. He sneaks over to the house and peers into the window. He sees* **WILLIAM** *poring over papers.*)

(We understand he is losing his shit a bit.)

(He removes some sort of listening device from his person and presses it against the window pane.)

WILLIAM. Focus	FBI MAN. Focus
Focus	Focus
Focus	Focus

(moments of listening)

(then:)

(**TREVOR** *enters.*)

I CAN'T FIND MY FORKS

WILLIAM. *(not looking up)* Oh hey, Killer

TREVOR. Sorry to interrupt –

WILLIAM. No, no

    Just stuck on this one chapter

    "The coadunation of barbarity and elegance

    In the work of Trevor Pratt"

    I feel like I can't actually unpack it

    Until I know more about your / current piece

TREVOR. William –

WILLIAM. I know, I know

    I'm not asking you to talk about it

    I'm just telling you why I'm stuck.

TREVOR. It's finished.

    (small beat)

WILLIAM. Finished-finished?

TREVOR. Yeah.

WILLIAM. Really?

    Oh my god

    When can I see it?

    Or should I wait for the opening?

    That might be better

    Or I could interview you now

    And then take a peek later

    Totally up to you

    Though to be honest

    I'm dying to see it

    No pressure

    None whatsoever

    *(****TREVOR**** retrieves a suitcase and hands it to ****WILLIAM****.)*

    What's this?

TREVOR. Shoes, shorts, socks, shirts, slacks
    Not your favorite corduroys
    you won't need them
    also they're disgusting and full of holes

WILLIAM. Is this for press?
    Or a quick vacay before the stampede?

TREVOR. I rolled your ipod in your green shirt
    you may want to take it out for the plane ride

WILLIAM. *(delighted)* Plane ride?
    Fancy!

TREVOR. Gum, batteries
    That book on sadism and aesthetics
    Lip balm
    Sunscreen

    I packed one for Randy too

WILLIAM. Randy's coming?
    Well gosh you're certainly thorough
    Where's your bag?

TREVOR. I'm not going

    *(**TREVOR** hands **WILLIAM** two plane tickets.)*

    (Reading tickets.)

WILLIAM. Puerto Rico?
    These are / open-ended tickets

TREVOR. *(cont.)* Your plane leaves tonight at 9

    *(**RANDY** storms in, panicked.)*

RANDY. I can't find my forks

TREVOR. They're in your suitcase

RANDY. Why are they in my suitcase
    Why were you in my room

TREVOR. You're going on an adventure

RANDY. For how long?

TREVOR. Hard to say

RANDY. Will I miss your opening?

TREVOR. Yes, / Randy

RANDY. This is BULLSHIT

This is BULLSHIT

She wants the spotlight all for herself

WILLIAM. Take a chill, pal

Nothing is in stone

We can all talk about this like rational / people

RANDY. I don't want an adventure!

I want to be on TV!

TREVOR. Randy –

RANDY. YOU HORRIBLE FREAKY BITCH.

I HATE YOU BOTH!!!!

FUCK YOU!!!!!!!!!!!

WILLIAM. Randy!

(He does a weird aggressive dance move. Then remains still.)

(beat)

WILLIAM. Muffin.

Look at me.

Is this about Melanie?

TREVOR. No –

WILLIAM. Had I known she'd be so *adhesive* / I would have never

TREVOR. This isn't about Melanie!

I don't want you here for my opening.

WILLIAM. Randy can handle it

His new therapist / seems to be wor–

TREVOR. It's YOU, William.

(small beat)

WILLIAM. Trev

When I let you use those photos of Diane

I took my hands off the wheel.

I signed up for this.

All of it.

TREVOR. *(suddenly vicious)* I'm, I'm sick.
Sick of your intellectual postscripts.
Your fame whoredom
Your cloying regard
And I'm so fucking sick
of being the one thing
that makes your career feel important.

(beat)

(WILLIAM *packs up his papers.)*

WILLIAM. If this is how you need to be supported, fine.
But you didn't need to say any of that.

*(**WILLIAM** exits with his suitcase. **TREVOR** is stricken. She has some sort of strange gasping breakdown. But she recovers. She sings the keeper of the marvel song to calm herself.)*

*(**FBI MAN** is beaming, glowing.)*

FBI MAN. *(warm, impressed)* The captain going down with her ship.
That's my girl.

*(**TREVOR** freezes.)*

(like a little kid)

God, I have so many questions!
Are you claustrophobic?
Are you a meticulous self-groomer?
Do you enjoy scalding hot showers?
Do you get impatient with slow drivers?
Do you abide by the following tenets:

FBI MAN. *(cont.)* Strictness, diligence, decisiveness?
Do you think cruelty is the only true universal language?

And more and more and more!
Gaps to fill, dots to connect...

And maybe you'll want to know about me too?

"Who is this bloodhound who's been tracking me?

Where does he go at night?
How many languages does he know?"
(Seven.)
"What is his moral imperative?"
(To serve my country.)
"What does he look like naked?"
(A stallion.)

(**FBI MAN** *giggles. But then. He frowns.*)

What am I saying?
Snap out of it, man
You're a professional
Claim yourself
Who are you?
Who are you?

(He does some martial arts.)

You are
The last of a dying breed

Get the job done.
Get it done, asshole.
Make her fear you.
Make her fear herself.
Make her sizzle in the hot white beam of your righ-
teousness.
And admit defeat.

(refreshed)

Ladies and gents
The time is nigh

The interview to end all interviews

(spotlight on **TREVOR***)*

FBI MAN. *(cont.)* Trevor Pratt
30
Primary subject of observation
Achieved a cultish following for a photo series
Poor eating habits

No siblings
Mother was a journalist
Father was a hair model
Has tiny hands and an avid mouth

(Does an incredible, eerie impression of **TREVOR**.*)*

"I said 'don't touch the art'

My hands were like this the whole time
Tell me you can handle it
Buy a bright red belt
This is going to hurt like a motherfucker

You'll be rewarded
When the doors are flung open"

*(***FBI MAN*** changes into a bumbling reporter outfit.)*

*(***TREVOR*** appears on the screen. She is nervous. She is putting on make-up and fixing her hair.)*

Dolling herself up
Like a little painted peanut

*(***FBI MAN*** is uncharacteristically nervous.)*

(He wipes his hands on his slacks.)

Sweaty. Jeez. Okay.

(He emboldens himself.)

Focus. And.

(He enters.)

A STRAW MIGHT HELP

*(***TREVOR***'s studio. A new piece is in the center of the room, covered in a tarp.)*

(a knock)

TREVOR. It's unlocked

*(***FBI MAN*** enters. ***TREVOR*** is busy fussing around the room, preparing, and does not fully register him at first.)*

Welcome

Would you like some coffee?

It's strong

So strong your ends will split

FBI MAN. That will be fine.

(She scurries off to get coffee.)

TREVOR. Thank you for coming all the way up here

I know it's a long drive

Making *The New York Times* come to me, what a shitbag I am…

The photographers are on their way too

I just got a text

(She brings him a cup and takes a long drink of coffee herself. Most of it dribbles down her chin.)

FBI MAN. Um…

TREVOR. Excuse me

I usually drink it iced.

FBI MAN. That happens a lot?

TREVOR. I can't feel my face anymore

FBI MAN. Oh.

A straw might help

TREVOR. Good idea.

(Then, it dawns on her.)

You're not my *Times* reporter…

(He smiles. She gasps.)

TREVOR. *(cont.)* It's you.

The exterminator

(Thunderclap, or the dramatic equivalent.)

FBI MAN. It is I.

TREVOR. Okay

I've been waiting for this –

FBI MAN. Not so fast.

I have a few questions

TREVOR. Of course you do

(He circles her like an animal. He wants to enjoy this moment. Take his time. Relish her fear.)

FBI MAN. Trevor Pratt

Famous artist

Loved by many

Feared by none

Is that your goal?

To make people fear you?

TREVOR. No

FBI MAN. Then?

TREVOR. I want to make the reality of my culture conscious of itself

FBI MAN. How

TREVOR. By confronting the transgressive nature of modern spectatorship

In regards to human anguish

FBI MAN. That's a mouthful.

TREVOR. Are you being deferential or condescending?

FBI MAN. Does it matter?

TREVOR. Only if you care what I think of you.

FBI MAN. I do if it affects what you tell me.

TREVOR. Then I choose neither.

FBI MAN. Ho ho…

Too bad *I'm* the one calling the shots here

(He moves in quick, like a fox.)

FBI MAN. *(cont.)* Here's a fun question
Why do you want people to die?

TREVOR. I don't
I want them to feel the *potential*

FBI MAN. But these animals are lethal

TREVOR. How do you know?
They weren't tested

FBI MAN. Don't be coy
You've been injecting them –

TREVOR. With painkillers
That's not illegal

FBI MAN. You lie!
One human being has perished from contact!
Maybe more!

TREVOR. The animals *may* be infected
But they may not
I wouldn't know
I found them on the side of the road.

(Beat. **FBI MAN** *turns to us.)*

FBI MAN. Pause a moment here.

So crafty!
Much taller in person
Her fingers are longer too
The curve of her back –

TREVOR. Un-pause

FBI MAN. Agk –
How did you –

TREVOR. (…)

(Nevermind. Now he means business.)

FBI MAN. Alright, Angelface
Let's have a dose of straight talk.
1) You have compromised the health and security of
our nation

FBI MAN. *(cont.)* 2) You have committed acts of biological
warfare

3) You are a terrorist

4) You will be in prison for a very very long time

TREVOR. You don't have anything on me

FBI MAN. I don't *need* anything

I have ways of making people talk

(He tries his eye trick on **TREVOR.** *But somehow it
doesn't work. She advances on him.)*

TREVOR. What makes you think you deserve to be here

Seeing what I've built

Feeling things I let you feel

Becoming part of my story

(He tries it again. No go.)

FBI MAN. *(to us, panicking re: his eye trick)* It isn't working

(to her)

Just who do you think you are?

*(***TREVOR*** smiles.)*

TREVOR. I am the keeper of the marvel.

(Somehow, she reverses the eye's effect. The **FBI MAN**
begins to wither. The room changes.)

FBI MAN. I had a vegetable garden when I was twelve

It was infested with grubs

I'd brush them gently off the leaves

Then collect them in tin foil

and let them loose outside

Six years later I joined the army

Got sent to the Gulf

Nine years after that

I was rollerblading in my neighborhood

I rolled over a caterpillar

Saw its guts explode from one of its sides

TREVOR. You saw its guts
    You were riding pretty slowly

FBI MAN. It was on purpose.

TREVOR. Do you ever want to punish others
    For things you find horrible in yourself?

FBI MAN. Every day.

(She runs her fingers along his eyepatch.)

TREVOR. I know why you lost this eye

FBI MAN. Why?

(She flips the eyepatch up.)

TREVOR. Because you're a patriot.

(She strokes his scar throughout the following.)

(quietly) They used the prongs of a dirty dinner fork
After eating a meal of roasted lamb

You were so hungry
You remember the smell of the meal
More than the pain

The one who did it
Was the kindest of the three
He moved quickly
And avoided the lid
So you could close it afterwards

They threatened to cook it and feed it to you
But they didn't want you to gain strength from the eating
So they fed it to their dogs
While you watched

When you were rescued by your men
They gave you the privilege of avenging yourself
Which you did
One by one
In private

And
You took your fucking time

(Beat. The room changes back. **FBI MAN** *is a little lost.)*

TREVOR. *(cont.)* Now I want you to tell me something else.

FBI MAN. Okay

TREVOR. I want you to say it quietly

FBI MAN. Okay

TREVOR. And I don't want you to look at me as you say it

FBI MAN. Okay

>   *(beat)*

>   *(***TREVOR*** *pulls the tarp from the final piece of art.* **MELANIE** *is strapped to the metal, dying.)*

TREVOR. How.

FBI MAN. I –

>   I told her to touch them

TREVOR. Why?

FBI MAN. For you.

>   *(beat)*

TREVOR. There are about fifty photographers outside that door

>   It's not too late to disappear

>   *(small beat)*

FBI MAN. My loyalty to my vocation

>   My years of alienation and solitude

>   Suddenly

>   They're here

>   Two feet behind me

>   And you

>   You're eleven inches in front of me.

>   I've been living my life for this very moment.

>   *(Beat.* **FBI MAN** *does not help* **MELANIE.***)*

TREVOR. So have I.

(**TREVOR** *flings open the door of the shed. The* **PAPARAZZI** *begins snapping shots of the scene. Flashbulbs pop maniacally.*)

(**TREVOR** *smiles for the cameras and holds her arms out.*)

(*After a beat,* **FBI MAN** *also smiles for the camera.*)

CODA: A WAITIN'

(Eventually, **TREVOR** *and* **FBI MAN** *disappear.)*

(Lights change. **MELANIE** *and the* **ANIMALS** *sing this final song.)*

MELANIE & THE ANIMALS.

I dream of a villa on an Italian coast
wrought iron
white muslin
flowers
a tree

An outdoor dinner table with chairs for two
white marble
wine glasses
linens
and me

I dream the chairs are overturned
The glasses not filled
The wine not chilled

And there I sit
In my summer gown
a-waitn'
a-waitin'
a-waitin'…

A-waitin'…for you….

(blackout)

End of Play

"... raw, unusual, and exciting. *Roadkill Confidential* fits that mold, lightly borrowing from the narrative conventions of a noir flick to examine the intersections of art and violence... The show is funny, original, and intriguing... Callaghan uses a lot of illusion-shattering tricks in her script... *Roadkill Confidential* is a work of art..."
— *That Sounds Cool Blog*

"Trevor is the stereotypical tortured and misunderstood artist, unable to satisfyingly connect with her lover or anyone else. In real life such people tend to be tiresome, but Trevor... is written and played so well (by Sheila Callaghan and Rebecca Henderson respectively) that she's unceasingly interesting to watch..."
— *Show Showdown Blog*

"...an intriguing new play... [a] tense comedy-drama about the blurred line between media and message, art and life."
— *Blogcritics.org*

"Each moment in *Roadkill Confidential* is exquisitely crafted, stunning in both its heady intellectual content and its vivid, vibrant theatrical construction... it's all crystal clear and compelling, with a dry macabre sense of humor... if you like intellectually compelling and skillfully crafted theatre you should totally see it..."
— *Theatreiseasy.com*

"Sheila Callaghan's *Roadkill Confidential* is a charged collision of two, three, or maybe infinitely more, worlds... The real treat is the jungle gym of language on which [the characters] play. It is at once pipe-strong and improvisational, propulsive and obtuse, irreverent and heroic... Callaghan perfectly supports the layers of this spicy delight with balanced notes that provide a full bodied, mysterious, and intoxicating potion."
— *deanpoyner.com*

"Callaghan has a wonderfully smart-aleck sensibility."
— *Chicago Tribune*